P9-CRT-673

MAR 2008

Tomie dePaola's

Front Porch Tales & North Country Whoppers

G. P. PUTNAM'S SONS

For all my Vermont and New Hampshire friends,
especially Steve A., Nannie, Jill and Steve C., Stephanie, Amanda,
Barbara, Barbie, Connie, Peggy, Timmie, Nancy, Janet and David,
McGuff, those monk fellas, Bern and Peter, Kelly, Andrea, Philip
(and their better halves), and without a doubt, Bob.

Special thanks to Sherry Litwack, Julie Cummins, Patrick Hart,
Caroline Litwack, Michaela May, and John Peters, who helped
with the initial research for an American folktale book.

And, of course, to all those toothless "fahmahs" and big-bosomed
"womin" who were so good to me when I was a "youngstah."

G. P. PUTNAM'S SONS

A division of Penguin Young Readers Group.

Published by The Penguin Group.

Penguin Group (USA) Inc., 375 Hudson Street, New York, NY 10014, U.S.A.

Penguin Group (Canada), 90 Eglinton Avenue East, Suite 700, Toronto, Ontario, Canada M4P 2Y3 (a division of Pearson Penguin Canada Inc.).

Penguin Books Ltd, 80 Strand, London WC2R 0RL, England.

Penguin Ireland, 25 St. Stephen's Green, Dublin 2, Ireland (a division of Penguin Books Ltd.).

Penguin Group (Australia), 250 Camberwell Road, Camberwell, Victoria 3124, Australia (a division of Pearson Australia Group Pty Ltd).

Penguin Books India Pvt Ltd, 11 Community Centre, Panchsheel Park, New Delhi - 110 017, India.

Penguin Group (NZ), 67 Apollo Drive, Mairangi Bay, Auckland 1311, New Zealand (a division of Pearson New Zealand Ltd).

Penguin Books (South Africa) (Pty) Ltd, 24 Sturdee Avenue, Rosebank, Johannesburg 2196, South Africa.

Penguin Books Ltd, Registered Offices: 80 Strand, London WC2R 0RL, England.

Copyright © 2007 by Tomie dePaola.

All rights reserved. This book, or parts thereof, may not be reproduced in any form without permission in writing from the publisher, G. P. Putnam's Sons, a division of Penguin Young Readers Group, 345 Hudson Street, New York, NY 10014.

G. P. Putnam's Sons, Reg. U.S. Pat. & Tm. Off. The scanning, uploading and distribution of this book via the Internet or via any other means without the permission of the publisher is illegal and punishable by law. Please purchase only authorized electronic editions, and do not participate in or encourage electronic piracy of copyrighted materials. Your support of the author's rights is appreciated. The publisher does not have any control over and does not assume any responsibility for author or third-party websites or their content. Published simultaneously in Canada.

Manufactured in China by South China Printing Co. Ltd. Design by Cecilia Yung and Gina DiMassi. Text set in ITC Biblon.

Library of Congress Cataloging-in-Publication Data De Paola, Tomie. Tomie dePaola's front porch tales and North Country whoppers / by Tomie dePaola. p. cm. Summary: A collection of folktales, original stories, and jokes reflecting the regional humor of northern New England. Contents: Inquirin' —Mud season — Mothah Skunk meets Sherman Curtis — Lookin' — Big Gertie and love at first sight — Countin' — Settin' — Bessie tells time — Wonderin' — The fahmah who hated wintah — Askin'. 1. Tales—New England. [1. Folklore—New England.] I. Title. PZ8.1.D43To 2007 398.2—dc22 [E] 2007017646 ISBN 978-0-399-24754-5

10 9 8 7 6 5 4 3 2 1

First Impression

Contents

Some of these stories were inspired by jokes or shaggy-dog stories I have heard over the years. Others are based on obscure folktales. A few are original with me, but would never have entered my imagination if I had not lived in Vermont and New Hampshire. (One actually happened to *me*, and I'll never forget it.)

My love affair with northern New England began one summer in 1947 when my parents took me and my two younger sisters to visit friends on Malletts Bay in Lake Champlain near Burlington, Vermont, for ten days.

We left home in Meriden, Connecticut, and drove up through the western part of the state into Massachusetts, traveling through beautiful, quaint towns such as Williamstown, Great Barrington and Stockbridge (home to Norman Rockwell), where the Berkshires hinted at the mountains to come in Vermont.

And sure enough, over the border in Vermont, the Green Mountains began. Majestic and greener than any twelve-year-old could imagine, they rose up out of corn-filled meadows dotted with calendar-perfect red barns. Outside of Manchester the mountains gave way to rolling dairy farmland filled with cows, and, before we knew it, Lake Champlain sparkled in the distance.

Ten magical days sped by.

I was up at the crack of dawn and out in the rowboat with mist rising from the lake, catching perch and cleaning it to fry for breakfast.

I discovered pepper steaks, a local treat served with French fries doused with malt vinegar instead of catsup.

Almost every day we bought fresh tomatoes and sweet corn at farm stands where, for the first time, I heard the old Vermont accent. *Aiyah* instead of "yeah"; *hewse* instead of "house"; *fahm* instead of "farm"; and *kews* instead of "cows." (If there are any North Country words that you don't understand, there's a glossary at the end of the book.)

On the way home, I secretly promised myself that one day I'd live in Vermont, or at least in New England. But it was as a young man in Weston, Vermont, that I had my true introduction to upper New England humor and their folk ways during my five years there.

It took a while to return for good, with Boston, Manhattan and San Francisco as side trips along the way. But in 1972 I moved back Northeast, settling in the Dartmouth–Lake Sunapee area of New Hampshire.

I've lived here ever since, but after more than thirty-five years, I'm still not a "local." There are rigid rules about these things. I'm not sure what they are, but it has something to do with having both great-grandparents born there, or nearby, to be considered "local." I once met a genuine New Hampshire native who explained that "jest cuz a cat has her kittens in the oven, it don't make 'em muffins."

So I'll never be a "muffin." Still, I don't mind being "that artist fella who writes books and lives up on County Road in that big place behind the gas station."

Tomie

New London, New Hampshire

2

Mud Season

Well sir, it happened one yehah during mud season.

Mud season. That's the time between wintah and spring when the cold and ice ooze up outta the ground and all the roads become a gooey mess, 'specially when they ain't bin paved ovah. Around heyah we say that the dang bottom falls out, and to tell ya the truth, that's exactly what it's like.

Now, Hiram Fullah, who lived right smack dab in the middle of the village, come out on his front porch to survey what was goin' on. It was pretty quiet, no folks, no wagons goin' down the main road cuz of the mud. Lord, theyah was a soupy mess where the road used to be.

All of a sudden-like, Hiram catches himself a glimpse of George Petty, the postman, comin' down the road. All Hiram could see stickin' outta the mud was George's head!

I reckon Hiram shouldn't a bin surprised to see George cuz everybody knows the postal system's motto: "Neither snow nor rain nor heat nor gloom of night stays these couriers from the swift completion of their appointed rounds."

I guess George Petty had decided that went fer mud, too.

Hiram called out to George, "Hey, theyah, George Petty. Whadda ya think you're doin'?"

"Whadda ya think? I'm deliverin' the mail," George answered.

Hiram shouted back, "Well, why doncha use your hoss?"

"I am," George replied. "I'm standin' on 'em!"

Mothah Skunk Meets Sherman Curtis

Sherman Curtis lived deep in the woods in a one-room tar paper shack. And it was a pretty good thing he did, too, what with all the wood smoke from a leaky stove, no runnin' water and jest a brook nearby. All that and the fact that he had never so much as touched a bar of soap. Sherman did smell a bit ripe. No respectable black fly or mosquito went near 'em.

In fact, when Sherman walked into town every spring to buy a new pair of overalls at the store, folks would rush to stand upwind of him. The storekeepah, Mistah Chadwick, would stick a clothespin on his nose and, standin' as far back as he could, hand Sherman a brand-new pair of overalls. Sherman would proceed to pull on the new pair right ovah the old pair. No tellin' how many layahs theyah were!

Well, this story ain't about the overalls. It's about the freak spring blizzard we had that yehah.

Sherman Curtis had jest left the store when,

without so much as a warnin', a killah blizzard blew down from the Northeast. In minutes the temperature dropped to below zero and the snow blew so hard, ya couldn't even see yer hand in front of ya. Most folks made it into their homes real quick except fer Sherman Curtis. He had a long walk back through the woods to his shack. He wandered and wandered, but the more he wandered, the more lost he was. It was a good thing, too, that he had on so many layahs of overalls cuz they kept him a little bit warm.

Then it got dark. And jest when Sherman Curtis had about given up hope, he bumped right into the front door of Mrs. Cave's house. "Go 'round to the side and ya can stay in the shed," Mrs. Cave told Sherman. "I'll leave a lamp in theyah and ya can build yerself a fire in the old stove." (Truth is Mrs. Cave was a kindhearted womin. She jest didn't want Sherman stinkin' up her nice house.)

The shed was small but tight. Theyah were some sacks filled with stuff that would make a nice soft bed, and a woodstove that heated it up real quick. So Sherman Curtis was even more comfortable than he woulda bin in his shack and soon he was asleep, snorin' like a buzz saw.

As often as it is with these spring blizzards, the snow stopped jest as quickly as it had started. The sky cleared and the temperature began to rise.

Now, it so happened that theyah was a mothah skunk and her three kits hibernatin' under the shed at Mrs. Cave's. What with the warm from the woodstove, the temperature comin' up and a full moon bustin' light into the sky, Mothah Skunk woke up.

Phew! What a smell! Mothah Skunk woke up her kits.

"Let's git outta heyah," she sniffed. "No skunk alive is a match fer Sherman Curtis."

SUMMER

Big Gertie and Love at First Sight

If ya are ever in Weston, Vermont, and ya drive north through the village on Route 100, you'll come to the Greendale Road on yer left. The beginnin' part is paved, but as soon as ya git to the unpaved part, you'll be drivin' into the Green Mountain National Forest.

Eventually, the road jest ends. Oh, ya can turn 'round all right, so no need to worry. But, at about the place where the road stops, to the left is a hill that used to have two tracks up it. They've probably overgrown by now, but at one time, those tracks was the loggin' road up the hill to the loggin' camp right smack dab at the top.

It was a pretty busy loggin' camp, too, if ya can believe what the old-timers do tell.

This is how the loggin' camp worked. All the trees were cut in the fall, when the leaves were lettin' go. Then, when the snow fell, most of the men went back into town. The men who were left workin' would hitch up the oxen and drag the logs out of the deep woods to the camp. Mud season would put a stop to the draggin', so the men worked real hard to beat the mud.

And then was the sugarin'. When the sugah maple's sap began to run in the early spring, most of the men would go help out the fahmahs in their sugah bush, tappin' the trees, gatherin' sap and boilin' it down. The fahmahs were always grateful fer the extra help. Sugarin' is no easy task, believe me!

Well, let's git back to the loggin' camp. Once the sugarin' was done and mud season was ovah, all the men that worked at the loggin' camp returned. Now it would be called the lumbah camp, cuz what the men would do is set up the sawmill and the crosscut saws to cut all the logs into planks that could be used fer buildin'. That would take all spring, all summah and into the beginnin' of fall.

First thing to do was to clean out the bunkhouse where the lumbahjacks had lived all wintah. The woodstove was cleaned out of all the ashes; all the winders was opened to git some fresh air in. The beddin' was hung out and whacked with sticks to git all the wintah dirt out and to fluff up all the feathers and scare away any critters that mighta moved in durin' the freezin' weather.

Next, they set up the cook tent and put together the big cookstove. After all, when the sawmill got goin' theyah'd be a big bunch of hungry men to feed. Other tents got put up: a dinin' tent with long tables and benches, a couple a extra sleepin' tents and a separate tent fer the cook.

The lumbahjacks were lucky. Fer two yehahs now, the cook had bin Big Gertie Benson from down in the village. Now, Big Gertie was BIG and TALL and BIG-BONED. Her whole family was that way and she had a bunch of cousins on her mothah's side that lived in the Midwest and were practically giants! They was the Bunyan family.

Big Gertie had the kindest heart in the whole world and she was one of the hardest workers in the Green Mountain State—some say in all of New England. Durin' the wintah, she kept house fer her widdered pa and three brothers. Since they all worked at the lumbah camp, Big Gertie follered them up the hill and cooked. And cook she did. She made biscuits so light, they floated an inch off the plate. No one baked a ham like Big Gertie, not to mention her turkey with all the fixins. And I don't know how she did it, but her baked beans were "gasless," if ya know what I mean.

Big Gertie's specialty was her flapjacks. Every Saturday and Sunday mornin', she'd whup up a batch of batter with eggs, stone-ground flour, a little cornmeal, a few other ingredients and plenty of buttermilk in a big jug. She'd set the jug, with a cloth ovah it, on a rock warmed by the sun. Then she'd build a fire under the big round saw blade that was too dull to use to cut wood. When the blade got hot, Big Gertie would sprinkle drops of water on it. If the water drops danced like crazy, the blade was ready. Big Gertie would pour the batter and, as quick as a wink, a stack of the most delicious flapjacks ya could imagine reached up ovah a foot high. And they were gone in a flash. Big Gertie kept cookin' and the men kept eatin'. Big Gertie's flapjacks and a cup of coffee were all ya needed to git goin' on a Saturday or Sunday mornin'.

Since Sunday was the Sabbath and no work was allowed, the lumbahjacks would set around and gab and mend their socks or whittle a little toy fer a nephew or a niece or git someone to write a letter home fer them. The only one who seemed to work seven days a week was Big Gertie.

"Ya know, men," the boss said, "we oughta find Big Gertie some help so's she can have a day off! Why, Sundays, she works harder than ever."

"But Boss," the lumbahjacks said, "no one can cook a turkey dinner like Big Gertie. It wouldn't feel like Sunday without our turkey dinner. Maybe Big Gertie would like some other day off—like Monday or Tuesday."

So, the boss spoke with Big Gertie and it was decided that Big Gertie would work only five days, includin' Sunday. She'd have Monday and Tuesday off, she would have an assistant "cookie," and she'd git the same pay as always. But she had to find the assistant.

Big Gertie started down the loggin' road to the village fer a look-see, but before she got down the hill, guess who she met a-comin' up the road? Seth Parkhurst from Londonderry. He had heard that they needed some volunteers to help set porky-pine traps to catch them critters that was girdlin' the trees.

Now, Seth Parkhurst was right puny with long skinny arms and legs, big ears that stuck out like handles on a pitchah, and a little red nose perched right above a walrussy mustache.

Big Gertie took one look at Seth and fell smack dab in love.

"Can ya cook?" she asked him.

"Aiyah. Not so good as I hear ya can," Seth answered. "But I can learn fast."

"Would ya mind workin' fer a womin?" Big Gertie asked with a blushin' smile.

Seth Parkhurst blushed back. "I'd be real happy workin' fer you!" he said softly.

I guess ya could say that it was love at first sight. So up to the lumbah camp went Big Gertie Benson and Seth Parkhurst to cook up a storm. Oh, the meals that come outta that cook tent! Plattahs of fried eggs, thick-cut bacon, flapjacks, fried lumbahjack mush and towers of toast fer breakfast. Ham sandwiches, deviled eggs, succotash and potato salad fer lunch. Ham steaks, pot roast, turnips, roast potatoes, cream gravy and at least two kinds of pie fer suppah. Those lumbahjacks were in seventh heaven the same as their cooks.

Big Gertie never did git her day off. Theyah they was, seven days a week, three meals a day. When the boss mentioned it to Big Gertie, she replied, "Oh, I'm only helpin' him out till he gits the hang of it."

And of course, Seth didn't take no day off neither. "Big Gertie likes it when I help her out," he'd say.

One Sunday, Big Gertie and Seth surprised everyone with one big flapjack that covered the big round saw blade. Everyone sat around it and dug in. It became a Sunday tradition a sorts, along with beans and franks and brown bread fer Saturday suppah, roast turkey with all the fixins fer Sunday, fried chicken fer Wednesday suppah and always good breakfasts so the lumbahjacks could saw up lots of boards.

One day in the late summah, when the work was pretty much caught up, the camp decided to have an afternoon of games. Ya know, like a log-splittin' competition, an ax-throwin' contest and a crosscut saw race.

"Ah, come on, Seth," Big Gertie said. "It'll be fun."

"But Gertie," Seth answered, "I'm too puny. I'll never be able to keep up with ya."

"Never ya mind," Big Gertie said. "Jest ya do what I tell ya and we'll win, you'll see!"

The day of the games came and soon it was time fer the crosscut saw race. Theyah were fouah teams: John Parker and Alvin Austin, Lonnie Benson (Big Gertie's brother) and Lampson Tyler, Harrison Benson (Big Gertie's other brother) and Silas Kidder, and of course, Big Gertie Benson and Seth Parkhurst.

The first three teams did pretty well, with Harrison and Silas havin' a slight lead.

Now it was Big Gertie's and Seth's turn.

"Whadda I do, Gertie?" Seth whispered.

"Ya jest hold on tight to your end of the saw and I'll do the rest," Big Gertie whispered back.

One, two, three. Big Gertie began to push and pull the saw, back and forth, back and forth across the log. Seth hung on as he went swingin' through the air like a mad thing.

"An' the winner is . . . Big Gertie Benson and Seth Parkhurst."

"Hurray!" the lumbahjacks shouted.

"But ya did all the work, Gertie," Seth said.

"But ya hung on, Sethie," Gertie said back.

Well, the lumbah camp lasted a few more yehahs and then as they usually do, it moved on, farther north up around Pittsford.

It was then that Big Gertie Benson and Seth Parkhurst decided to tie the knot. Big Gertie's father and brothers moved out of the house, followin' the loggers north. And it wasn't too long, maybe a yehah, before twins were born to Big Gertie and Seth: a boy, big-boned and tall jest like Gertie, and a skinny girl jest like Seth.

Ovah the yehahs they had a pahcil of kids, half of 'em big and half of 'em puny. They all got along real well and they all eventually married real well, too. Before long theyah were cousins and Benson-Parkhursts all ovah the place.

Big Gertie Benson and Seth Parkhurst had one of those fairy-tale lives together. They truly lived happily ever after. And every once in a while, to celebrate how they met, Big Gertie would git out the saw blade and make the biggest flapjack ya ever seen!

FALL

SETTIN'

I know this is a true story cuz a friend of mine knew these two young fellas livin' in an old fahmhouse out theyah on the Greendale Road and they told him about the night they was invited to a set, and he told me.

They was livin' what they called "the simple life." They heated the fahmhouse with wood and ate real simple, bakin' their own bread and stuff like that. They did some artwork and some weavin'. They was real good friends with those monk fellas that lived up County Road in a place called the Priory.

Now, one of the locals had taken those monks—and the two fellas—under his wing. That was Frank Stevens. He and two of his sons helped the monks

out with buildin' a barn and takin' care of the kews. Frank showed 'em how to tap their sugah maples so's they could make maple syrup to sell. Frank and his wife, Maude, lived on Route 100 in a kinda ramshackle house. The two sons had small houses

on the same property. Theyah was always a bunch of dogs around and the yard was mostly filled with old car pahts and old tractahs.

One day, Frank stopped by the fellas' house with an invite.

"Maude and I would like it if ya two fellas would come and set with us on Saturday evenin', 'round seven—after suppah."

The fellas accepted, feelin' it was quite a compliment to be invited.

They arrived exactly at seven. Another car was settin' in front of Frank's house.

The light was on ovah the kitchen door. (The front door that went into the pahlah was only used fer weddins or funerals.) Frank answered their knock and right into the kitchen they went. Theyah was fouah kitchen chairs set up in a neat row. One of the chairs was taken by Lonnie Fullah, an old friend of Frank's who lived farther up Route 100. It was his car that was settin' outside.

Mrs. Stevens—Maude—was perched on a stool next to the big black iron cookstove. She was feedin' kindlin' into it. On the other side of her was a small kitchen table covered with a clean dish towel. Somethin' was risin' underneath it. Maude had the ar-ther-i-tis pretty bad, so she didn't move around too much.

Maude nodded greetin' to the fellas. She didn't say nothin' though. The same with Lonnie Fullah. The two fellas sat down on the chairs Frank pointed at.

They all set. The stove crackled and the kitchen clock ticked loudly.

They set some more. Maude moved on her stool and uncovered some dough on the table. She pulled a big pan of grease ovah to a hot spot on the stove. Then she began to cut and fry doughnuts.

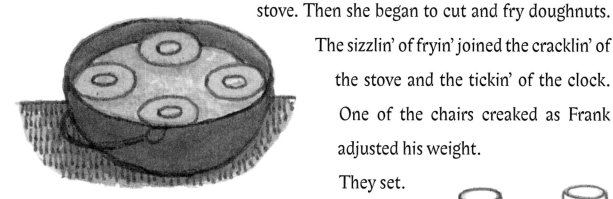

The sizzlin' of fryin' joined the cracklin' of the stove and the tickin' of the clock. One of the chairs creaked as Frank adjusted his weight.

They set.

Maude piled her tasty doughnuts on a plattah, and Frank passed 'em around, with some cidah. Nothin' was said.

They set and they set and they set.

The clock struck nine.

Lonnie stood up. "Well, thankee, Frank and Maude. Nice evenin'."

The two young fellas did the same. I hear they didn't say a word as they drove home.

On Monday, they saw Frank.

"Thanks fer comin'," Frank said. "Maude and I was sayin' that Saturday was one of the best sets we ever had."

Bessie Tells Time

Theyah is a story in the state of Maine about a rich lady who was driven 'round the state throwin' lupine seeds out the car's back winder. She wanted to make Maine a prettier place, and as sure as a lobstah has two claws (unless it's bin in a fight), she did. All ya have to do is to drive around Maine in the spring and you'll see fer yerself.

But theyah's a story about another rich lady drivin' 'round, too. I heard that this heyah rich lady was drivin' 'round the hills of Vermont to look at the fall folige.

Now, that don't seem at all unusual. Lots of people—men, ladies, children, rich and not quite so rich—pour into Vermont in the fall of the yehah to see the folige, cuz to tell ya the truth, theyah is nothin' else like it, 'less ya cross ovah into New Hampsha. It's the sugah maples that make the difference. They turn a special red-orange color that makes the mountains and hills in both places look like they got a lightbulb inside 'em.

But let's git back to the rich lady drivin' around lookin' at the folige. Ya see, she wasn't the one doing the drivin'. She was settin' in the backseat with her little doggie, givin' him doggie biscuits while she was drinkin' hot tea out of her thermos. The car was bein' driven by James. He was her showfur or some such name like that.

They had started out that mornin' in Great Barrington, Massachusetts, where the first tinges of leaf changes were happenin'. Then they drove right up Route 7 through Stockbridge, where the artist Norman Rockwell lived at one time. The colors of the folige grew more and more beautiful the more they headed north, and it wasn't unusual fer the lady to say, "James, stop here so you can take my picture against this magnificent vista." So theyah was a lot of stoppin' and startin'.

The car finally crossed the border into Vermont. The Green Mountain National Forest was the sight worth seein'.

The car continued on toward Manchester, where the rich lady wanted to stop at the famous Equinox House fer a nice luncheon and to "freshen up."

"Now, James," the lady said, looking up from her road map, "I suggest we continue up Route 7 until we reach Rutland. Then we can go on Route 4 all the way to Woodstock, where we will spend the night."

"Yes, madame," James answered.

More drivin', more photos. When they got near to Wallingford, more and more meadows filled with black-and-white cows began to appear.

"James," the rich lady said, "can you tell me what time it is? My wrist-watch seems to have stopped."

"Oh dear, madame," James answered. "It seems as though my pocket watch has stopped as well." The car didn't have a clock, believe it or not. It had a little vase with a rosebud in it by one of the back winders, but no clock.

Suddenly, as they came 'round a curve in the road, they saw a fahmah standin' by his fence.

"Stop, James," the rich lady said. "Perhaps that farmer can tell us what time it is."

"Yes, madame," James replied. He put the car in reverse and backed up to where the fahmah was. The lady rolled down her winder.

"My good man," she said a bit loudly. "Can you perhaps tell us what time it is?"

"Aiyah," the fahmah answered. "Jest let me git my kew." He walked a ways into the field and called, "Heyah, Bessie." A great big black-and-white Holstein cow came walkin' ovah to the fahmah, her cowbell ringin' loudly.

"Steady now," the farmah said. Bessie stood theyah as still as a Woody Jackson paintin'. (Woody paints a lot of black-and-white Vermont cows.)

The fahmah leaned down and looked right under that cow. "Good girl," he said as he stood up. The fahmah came back to the fence.

"It's exactly twenty minutes past two," he politely told the rich lady.

"Thank you, so much," the rich lady replied. She rolled up her winder and instructed James to drive on. As she was settin' her wristwatch, she suddenly sat straight up.

"James," she said, "did you see that? I have never, ever seen anything like that in my life. I must find out how that farmer did that! Back up!"

James backed up. The fahmah was still standin' by the fence. The rich lady got out.

"My good man," she said to the fahmah, "that was astonishing. Exactly how *did* you *do* that?"

"Well, ma'am," the fahmah said, "if ya climb ovah heyah, I'll show ya."

Between James and the fahmah, the rich lady got ovah the fence and into the meadow.

"Watch fer the kew pies," the fahmah warned.

When he and the rich lady got to the same spot as before, the fahmah called Bessie. The cow obediently ambled ovah.

"Steady now," the fahmah said. "Now, ma'am, if ya bend down and look right underneath Bessie's belly—

—ya can look right down to the village and see the clock on the church steeple."

WINTER

THE FAHMAH WHO
HATED WINTAH

The dividin' line between Vermont and New Hampsha is the Connecticut River. Most states or cities divided by a river have the boundary between the two places somewheres in the middle of the river.

Not so with Vermont and New Hampsha. New Hampsha owns the whole Connecticut River up to the shoreline on the Vermont side. So what happens, you're going to ask me, when theyah's a big flood and the river overflows its banks? Who pays the taxes on the land under the river? Well, to be honest, I can't tell ya that, cuz I jest don't know and I don't have the time to go to Concord or Montpelier to look it up in the state books. Too many chores to do.

But I do know this happened.

The town called White River Junction was right at the place where the White River, which is in Vermont, and the Connecticut River meet each other. Now, that caused a problem fer White River Junction cuz Vermont and New Hampsha were always arguing ovah the boundaries. So the town was always bouncing back and forth between the two states, 'specially whenever the state legislatures were mad at each other. Finally, or so I heard (don't hold me to it—I only heard it), the case went up to the Supreme Court of the United States so it could be decided once and fer all whether White River Junction was in New Hampsha or Vermont. Oh, theyah were agreements back and forth with all the lawyers havin' a really good old time yellin' at each other, *habeas corpus* this and *habeas corpus* that and *I object* and *objection overruled*. It was a high old time down theyah in Washington, D.C. Finally, the court made the decision. White River Junction was definitely in Vermont.

Since theyah weren't any television in those days, all the newsreel movie companies like Pathé and Movietone came roarin' up to interview the populace about the decision.

They were stoppin' people in downtown White River Junction and in Hanover, where Dartmouth College was. Everyone had an opinion, 'specially those Dartmouth boys—somethin' about not being able to take their dates across the state line to White River Junction anymore. (New Hampsha didn't have as many rules as Vermont.)

As one movie crew was leavin' the area, they saw Frank Lamson out shovelin' snow off his barn roof. The cars stopped. The movie folk got outta their cars and set up their cameras, lights and other equipment they had stored in their trunks.

The reporter asked, "Sir, may we ask you a couple of questions?"

"Aiyah," Frank said as he climbed off into the huge snow pile next to his barn roof.

"What state was your farm in yesterday?" the reporter asked.

"New Hampsha," Frank answered.

"Well, because of the courts," the reporter continued, "you now live in Vermont. How does that feel?"

"I'll tell ya," Frank said. "I'm right relieved. I don't think I coulda survived another one of those New Hampsha wintahs!"

Glossary

a	of	*mistah*	mister
aiyah	yes (yeah)	*mothah*	mother
ar-ther-i-tis	arthritis	*oughta*	ought to
bin	been	*outta*	out of
cidah	cider	*ovah*	over
cookie	cook	*pahcil*	parcel
coulda	could have	*pahlah*	parlor
cuz	because	*pahts*	parts
doncha	don't you	*pitchah*	pitcher
'em	him, them	*plattah*	platter
fahm	farm	*porky-pine*	porcupine
fahmah	farmer	*set*	sit
fahmhouse	farmhouse	*settin'*	sitting
fella	fellow	*showfur*	chauffeur
fer	for	*storekeepah*	storekeeper
folige	foliage	*sugah*	sugar
follered	followed	*summah*	summer
fouah	four	*suppah*	supper
Fullah	Fuller	*thankee*	thank you
git	get	*theyah*	there
Hampsha	Hampshire	*tractahs*	tractors
hewse	house	*whadda*	what do
heyah	here	*whup*	whip
hoss	horse	*widdered*	widowed
jest	just	*winder*	window
kew	cow	*wintah*	winter
kinda	kind of	*womin*	woman, women
killah	killer	*woulda*	would have
layahs	layers	*ya*	you
lobstah	lobster	*yehah*	year
lumbah	lumber	*yer*	your
lumbahjack	lumberjack	*yerself*	yourself
mighta	might have	*youngstah*	youngster

P9-CSB-459

To all the little flaws that make us so beautiful . . .
C.R.

Cataloging-in-Publication Data has been applied for and may be obtained
from the Library of Congress.

ISBN 978-1-4197-2823-5

Copyright © 2015 De La Martinière Jeunesse, a division of La Martinière Groupe, Paris
Text and illustrations copyright © 2015 Christine Roussey
English translation © 2018 Harry N. Abrams, Inc.

Originally published in French in 2015 under the title *Mon chien qui pue* by
Éditions de La Martinière, a division of La Martinière Groupe, Paris. This edition
published in 2018 by Abrams Books for Young Readers, an imprint of ABRAMS.
All rights reserved.

Printed and bound in France
10 9 8 7 6 5 4 3 2 1

Abrams Books for Young Readers are available at special
discounts when purchased in quantity for premiums and promotions
as well as fundraising or educational use.
Special editions can also be created to specification.
For details, contact specialsales@abramsbooks.com
or the address below.

ABRAMS The Art of Books
195 Broadway, New York, NY 10007
abramsbooks.com

My Stinky Dog

CHRISTINE ROUSSEY

Abrams Books for Young Readers

NEW YORK

This is Alfred.
He's the nicest dog around.
He's a great soccer player and my very best friend.

When my little sister lost her stuffed crocodile,
it was Alfred who found it.
One day, he even saved a fly from drowning.
Alfred follows me everywhere.
He'd never abandon me.
He's always there when I'm sad,
and he always cheers me up.

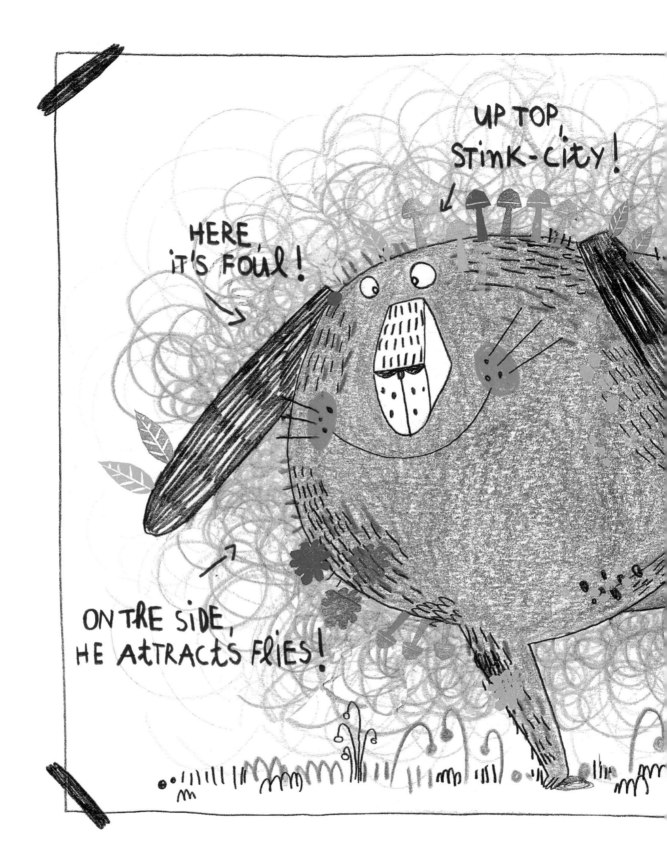

I love Alfred, but there's one little thing . . .
HE STINKS!
His feet stink, his ears stink.
His nose stinks, his back stinks, his belly stinks.

His left eye stinks, and his right eye stinks.
His whiskers and his tail stink.
From top to bottom, ALFRED STINKS!

He smells in the morning.
He smells in the afternoon.
He smells at night.

He smells on the couch.
He smells at the deli.
He smells at the library.
He smells at the pool.
He even smells at the supermarket!

I want to hug him, but . . . HE STINKS!
I'd love to read him stories, but . . . HE STINKS!
I wish I could bring him on trips with me, but . . . HE STINKS!

My family is moving to New York soon.
Will Alfred be allowed to come if he stinks like this?

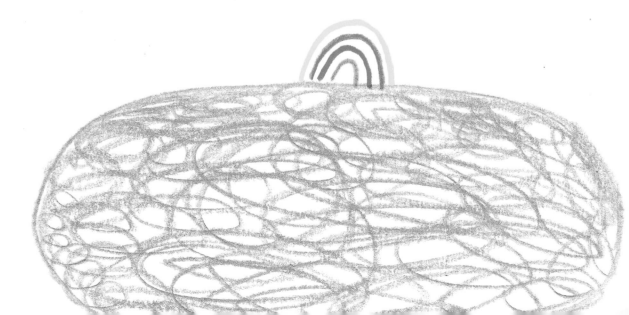

I tried spritzing him with perfume.

I hung pine-scented air fresheners around his neck.

I splashed him with my dad's aftershave.

BUT HE STUNK WORSE THAN BEFORE!

It was time to get serious!
First I lathered him. Then I soaked him.
Next I bubbled him. And bubbled him some more.
I rinsed him and dried him, and like magic . . .
ALFRED DOESN'T STINK ANYMORE!

He sparkles! He shines!
He smells clean and fresh, like wildflowers!
He smells so good now that his stink is gone!

The couch no longer smells like crushed kibbles.
The bed doesn't smell like moldy mud.
His whiskers don't smell like stale cheese,
and neither do his ears!

But now Alfred is acting strange.

Alfred wears boots and a raincoat in the
backyard to avoid the puddles and mud.
He brushes his teeth after each dog treat and sardine.
Alfred doesn't want to play anymore.
He's afraid to get dirty!

When Alfred isn't smelly, he's just not the same. So . . .

I bring Alfred outside without his boots or his doggy raincoat.
Belly to the ground, I roll in the mud until Alfred does, too!

We walk through the woods and smell the
mushrooms and crushed leaves.
We make a picnic with stinky cheese and tuna fish.

We sniff everything and we love it.
Everything is perfect in its own smelly way.
Just like Alfred.

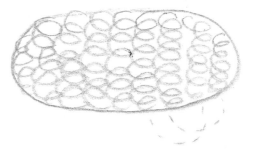

Tomorrow I'm leaving for New York with Alfred.
He's the nicest dog around.
He's a great soccer player and my very best friend.
And best of all . . . HE STINKS!